SIMON & SCHUSTER BOOKS FOR YOUNG READERS
An imprint of Simon & Schuster Children's Publishing Division
1230 Avenue of the Americas, New York, New York 10020
Text copyright © 2017 by Tim McCanna
Illustrations copyright © 2017 by Richard Smythe
SIMON & SCHUSTER BOOKS FOR YOUNG READERS is a trademark
of Simon & Schuster, Inc.
For information about special discounts for bulk purchases, please contact Simon & Schuster Special Sales
at 1-866-506-1949 or business@simonandschuster.com.
The Simon & Schuster Speakers Bureau can bring authors to your live event. For more information or to
book an event, contact the Simon & Schuster Speakers Bureau at 1-866-248-3049 or visit our website at
www.simonspeakers.com.
Book design by Chloë Foglia
The text for this book is set in Brioso.
The illustrations for this book are rendered in watercolor and finished digitally.
Manufactured in China
1116 SCP
First Edition
10 9 8 7 6 5 4 3 2 1
CIP data for this book is available from the Library of Congress.
ISBN 978-1-4814-6881-7
ISBN 978-1-4814-6882-4 (eBook)

For my parents, who took me
to lakes, rivers, and oceans
—T. M.

To my sisters, Liz and Kate
—R. S.

A Paula Wiseman Book
Simon & Schuster Books for Young Readers
New York London Toronto Sydney New Delhi

Watersong

Tim McCanna

Illustrated by
Richard Smythe

Drip

drop

plip

plop

pitter

patter

pat.

splutter

splatter

spitter

spatter

splat.

Splish

splosh

swish

slosh

squelch

squish

glop.

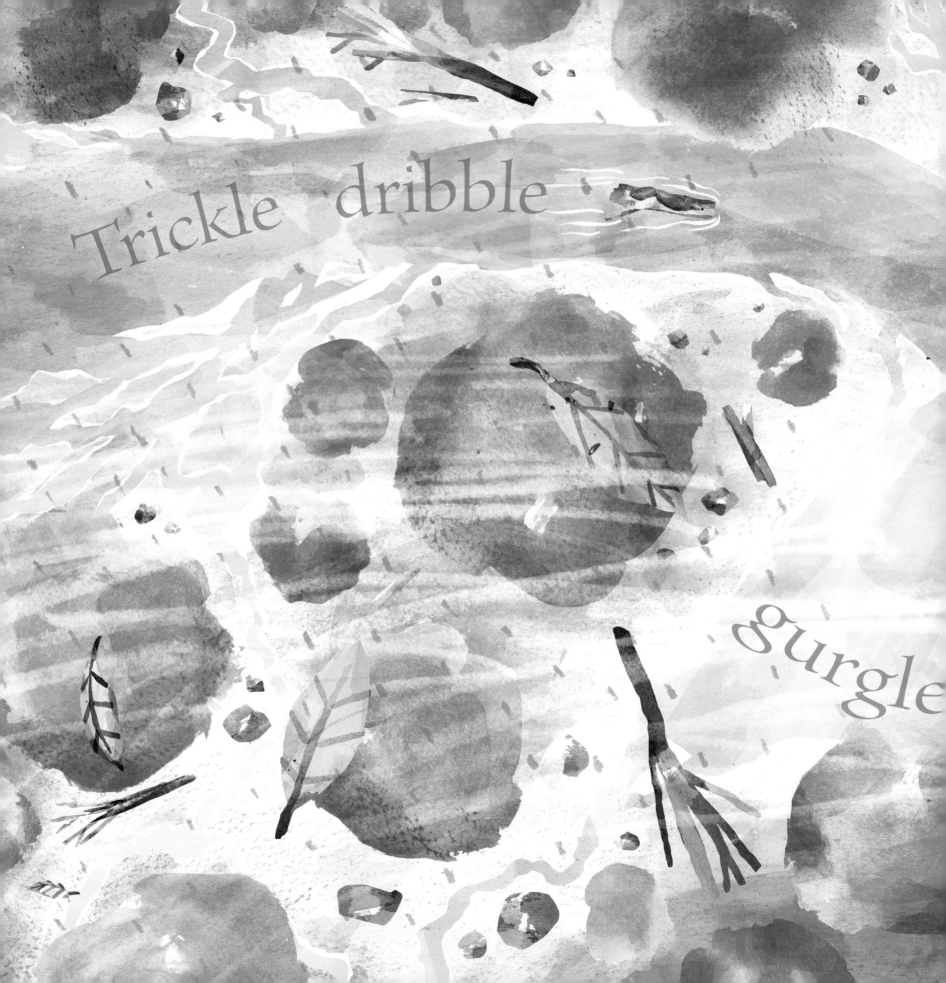

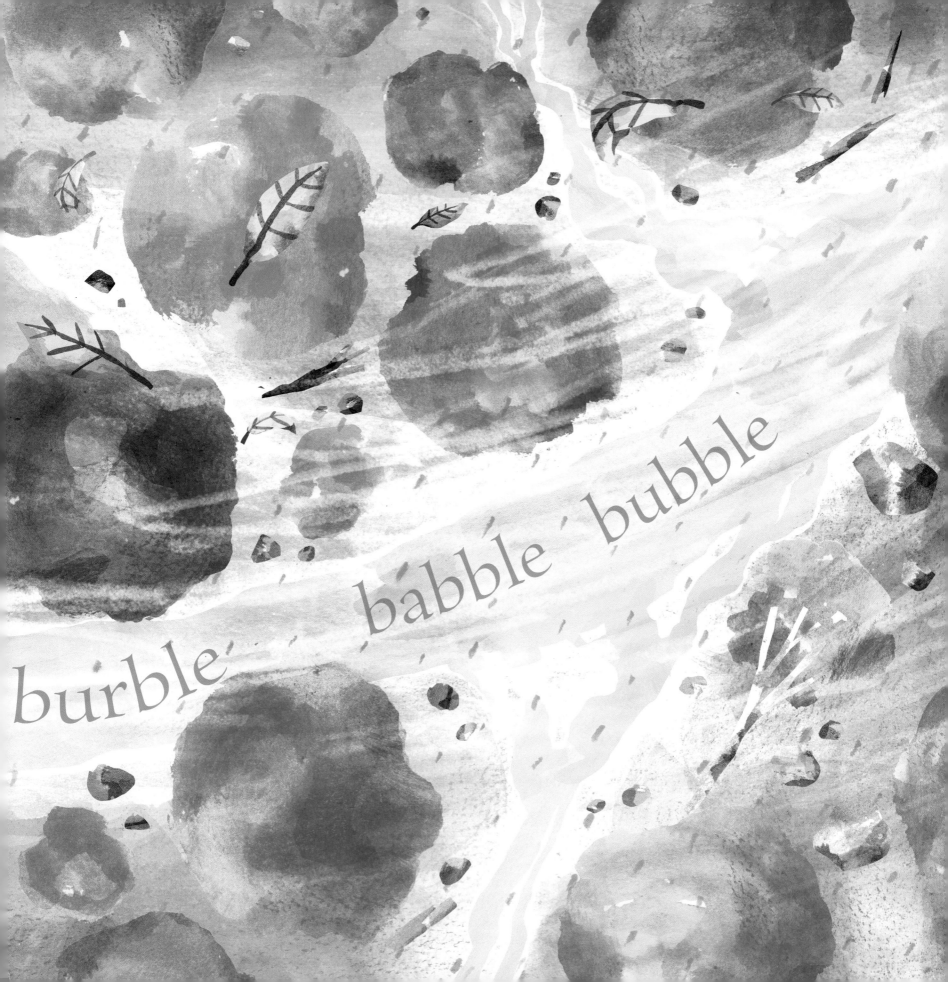

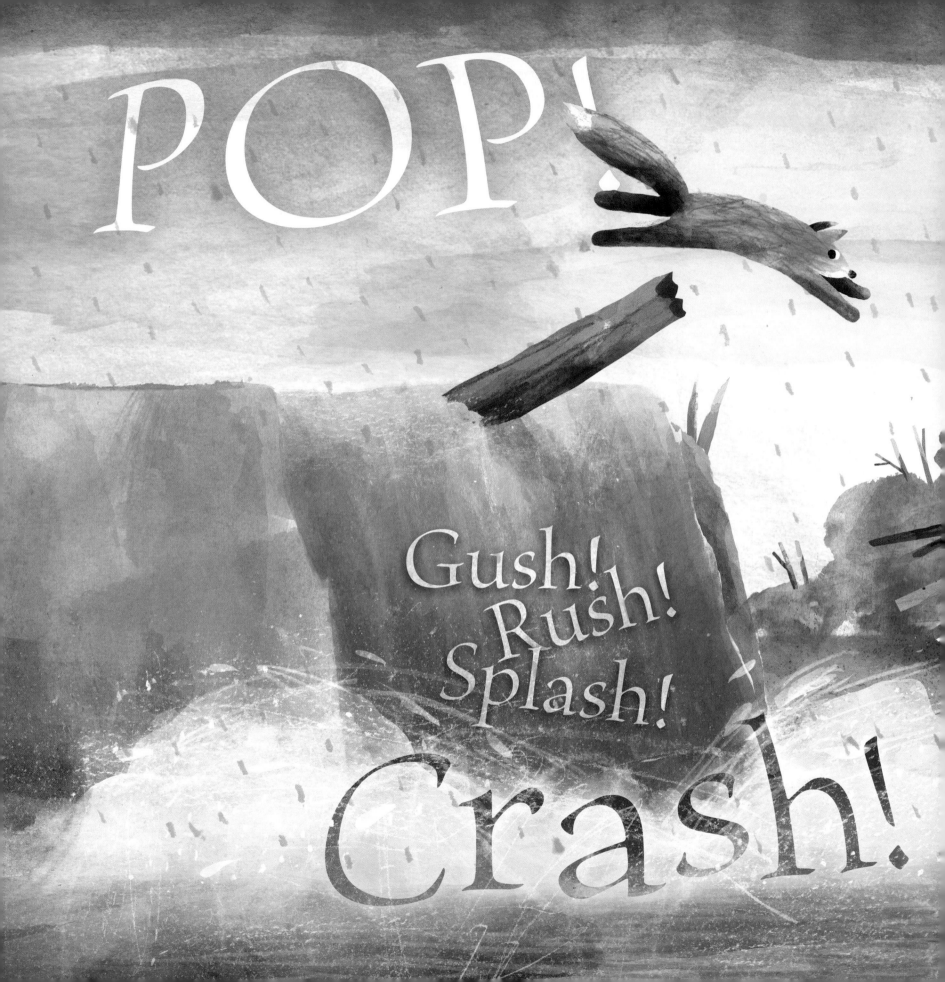

Whoosh sigh

whoosh sigh

sprout

bloom

grow.

Ripple shimmer

tumble glimmer

sparkle glitter

Listen to the Watersong

From the pitter-patter of raindrops to the roar of a river, water sings in harmony with the natural world. Water impacts animals, plants, land, and people in many ways. When you listen to the sounds of water, you can hear a song of life and connection.

• Foxes live in many different **habitats** around the world, from hot, dry deserts to cold, icy regions. The fox in this book lives in a forest habitat. Foxes are **omnivores**, which means they eat plants and animals. They have keen senses of hearing and smell, and can use their bushy tails like a blanket to keep warm. In a fox family, both parents care for their pups and take turns hunting for food.

• All plants, animals, and people live in a **watershed**, the land where water drains from a ridge top to a valley bottom. In a watershed, raindrops join to form a puddle. The puddle trickles down into a stream, which then flows into a river, and the river connects to the sea.

• An **ecosystem** is a community of living things and their physical environment. Plants and animals interact with each other and also with their surroundings. Whatever the size of the ecosystem, be it a puddle, cave, or prairie, each living or nonliving thing has a role to play.

• Many animals depend on **aquatic ecosystems** such as lakes, rivers, and oceans. Some creatures need the movement of water to survive. Others eat algae that grows in shallow ponds. Beavers can reshape streams with their dams, while trees shade the water where fish lay their eggs.

• Water travels back and forth from the sky to the ground in a process called the **water cycle.** When water heats up, it **evaporates**, becoming a vapor that floats upward. That floating water then **condenses** to form clouds. Once the water in the clouds is heavy enough, it **precipitates**, falling back to earth as rain or snow. Then the whole process starts over again.

• When light from the sun passes through water mist in the sky, a rainbow can occur. Droplets **refract**, or break up the light into seven separate colors that we can see—red, orange, yellow, green, blue, indigo, and violet. Water not only makes beautiful music, but it can paint too!